# HOOKED ON YOU

## A SWEET SMALL TOWN ROMANCE

## JACQUELINE WINTERS

Editor: Bridge to Story

Copy Editor: Write Girl Editing Services

Cover Design: BrennyLou Designs

*To my dad, who threw
the first fish I ever caught
back because it bit him.*

ky

"Sky, fix my tie?"

Sky Emerson inhaled a controlled breath, swallowing the pointed word, *Again?* before she faced the groom. When she first became a wedding planner, the job seemed like a dream, helping two people experience the most memorable day of their lives. Elaine, her boss and older sister, hadn't mentioned Sky would be retying an entitled groom's tie for the *fourth* time before the ceremony.

Sky turned and approached said groom, who towered over her by several inches. "Ken, you really need to leave the tie alone." She used the tone she might've picked for a three-year-old if she needed him to pay attention.

"Kenny, please," the groom corrected as she adjusted the tie straps hanging around his shoulders.

*Always smile.* Elaine's most important instruction and repeated piece of advice. *No matter what, always smile.*

"The ceremony starts in ten minutes. Don't undo this tie again." Her smile kept the groom at ease, but she hoped her tone's undercurrent was enough for him to leave it alone this time.

"It was crooked."

She took another deep breath. "Ken, I know you're nervous."

"Kenny."

Sky closed her eyes briefly to count to five. No time to try for ten. Maybe it was the hand she rested on his chest while she counted, or her failure to use her words that gave the wrong signal. Because at *four* Ken snaked his long fingers around Sky's cheek and smashed his lips to hers.

Sky's eyes shot open, but before she could push him away, the door flew open. A woman screamed. A camera lens flashed.

"Tammie, honey, you really shouldn't see—"

"She's trying to steal my husband! You harlot!" The icy look from the bride as she screamed was nothing in comparison to the fiery daggers in Sky's sister's eyes.

This was Elaine's business. She'd built Catching the Bouquet from the ground up, and this wedding was the most important of the entire season. Possibly of Elaine's career. The wedding of the mayor's daughter to the governor's favorite nephew. Members of two important political families whose union in holy matrimony was meant to cement a lifelong partnership and a mass of future voters.

"She threw herself at me," Sky heard Kenny claim, his hands finally dropping from her mortified face. He stumbled back into the wall, as though *he* were repulsed by *her*.

As people crowded in around the poofy princess gown, Elaine pushed into the room. A photographer continued to snap pictures, but Sky couldn't think of that now. She'd put up with the pompous groom for eight months. Endured insufferable sports jokes, pitiful attempts at flirting behind his fiancé's back, and needy tendencies that rivaled those of a spoiled toddler, all because it was the "biggest wedding of the year." Because of a five-thousand-dollar bonus and a chance at partner on the line—if only they survived today.

But none of that mattered now.

Having memorized the layout of the venue a week earlier, Sky darted for the side door tucked around a corner before Elaine and the nosy photographer could reach her. She slammed it shut, only temporarily drowning out the roar of outrage behind her.

Sky ducked behind the closest unlocked door, falling into a cleaning closet.

Enough was enough. Later, when she was home safe, she'd process all this over a bottle of chardonnay while she searched online for a new job. Because after the aftermath of that kiss, no matter who was at fault, she was surely going to need one.

But right now, what she needed most was an escape plan.

In the dimness, Sky dug her cell phone out of her dress and frantically scrolled for her best friend's number. "Colleen!"

"Skylar, this better be good. I'm in the middle of a hot stone pedicure—"

"The groom kissed me."

"That spoiled rotten brat, Kenny? The governor's nephew?"

"That's the one." Sky tried to slow her heavy panting, but with the scuttle of footsteps in the hallway, she couldn't hear whether it was working. "I'm trapped in a janitor's closet. Everyone's looking for me."

"I knew your sister should've dropped that couple," Colleen muttered. "I bet the jerk only used you to get out of marrying that bridezilla."

The sound of her best friend's voice—the laced humor in the most tense of situations—finally allowed Sky a moment of reprieve. "I don't know what to do, Coll. I rode here with Elaine. I'm all the way across town. In *heels*." Sky only wore heels to weddings. Her feet weren't cut out to slink across town in the dang things.

"Hang tight," Colleen ordered. "Don't leave that closet, you hear me?"

"Coll!"

"That's an order. I have a plan."

———

The minutes that lapsed in the dark corner of the janitor's closet felt like hours. Lemon oil fumes threatened to smother her, but Sky refused to budge, tucked behind a utility shelf full of mop buckets and cleaning gear. Elaine would never forgive her for this. The truth wouldn't matter.

Only perception mattered. Another nugget of survival advice in Elaine's business.

Sky let out a tiny screech when her phone lit up.

"Can you get to the back door?"

Bravely, Sky stood and dusted cobwebs from her lavender dress that surely sported some grease stains by now. "Let me check." She cracked the door just enough to spy a mob at the end of the wide hallway. In the thick of it stood a furious bride. At her side, Elaine in full dragon mode blocked Sky's best escape route. She pulled the door closed and whispered, "Not exactly."

"Then just get outside, any way you can," Colleen instructed. "My cousin Laney's in a silver Cavalier. She'll wait by the catering entrance. Ten minutes."

"What am I going to do, Colleen?"

"You're not coming home, sweetie."

"Elaine'll... What?"

"Laney and her husband are heading on a road trip. They're taking you with them."

"Where?"

"Small town. Vermont." Colleen didn't give Sky a chance to interject. "Not important. Sky, you're going to need to lay low for a while. The reporters alone will eat you alive for this scandal."

"Elaine's going to be crazy mad."

"For a while. We both know your sister. She'll overreact at first, but she'll cool off in time. Don't worry, I'll let Elaine know you're safe so she doesn't report you as kidnapped or something crazy." Colleen's voice sounded far away with that last bit. Sky imagined her checking the time on her phone. "They're pulling up in five minutes. Get out of that building!"

"Hold on." Sky snuck a second look down the hallway, her heart sinking. But then she spotted a window directly across the hall. A second story window.

She'd land in shrubbery.

"I'm going to murder her!" Sky didn't need the door cracked to know the exasperated outcry echoed down the hallway from a red-faced woman in the poofy princess gown. "Where is she?"

Though Sky feared the wrath of the almost-bride, it would be nothing in comparison to her sister's reaction. Elaine could make even the worst bridezillas look like spastic kittens.

"Sky?"

"I'm going for the window."

ky

"Let me try it one more time." The woman behind the check-in counter at the Sleepy Inn smiled and ran Sky's card through her ancient-looking swipe machine again.

Holding her breath as it decided her fate, Sky traced the scratch marks on the old wooden counter. *It has to work. It has to work.*

It was ten-thirty on a Tuesday night. This was the only inn in town. If her card was declined again, Sky'd have nowhere else to go. She didn't even have a car to sleep in. Colleen's cousin was miles away, staying at some family farm. And after that painful four-day road trip to Vermont, she'd rather face the hot-tempered bride-to-be than call that woman for help.

"I'm sorry, dear." The woman behind the register extended sympathetic eyes and a pitiful half smile. "Still declined."

Sky dug deep into the recesses of her purse, hoping to find a miracle. "Let me see if I have my other card with me." She didn't have another card, but she was hoping one might magically appear as she unloaded the largest contents and plopped them on the counter—a worn book she'd read two and a half times during that dreadful drive, a Nikon camera, and magazines.

"You have an awful lot of travel flyers." The woman glanced at the slipping stack piled there. Nodding to a brochure holder filled with the best attractions in little Monroe Falls, Vermont, she added, "Nearly as many as us."

Sky had a side hobby of coordinating honeymoons for Elaine's couples. She'd planned to spend what remained of last weekend scoping out the perfect little getaway for their first couple in the spring. A couple Sky would never be in contact with again. Maybe she could find a job as a travel agent.

"Planning some future trips," she finally said, her eyes drawn to the brochures. She reached for one about a pumpkin patch called Fall Into Pumpkins. "What an adorable name," she murmured.

"You certainly have the camera for traveling."

The Nikon was Sky's first love; they'd been together for five years. She'd bought it while in college, taking an extra job as a bartender to afford it. But she'd been hoping to upgrade to the latest model with the bonus she'd now never see. *Dang it, Ken.*

"You simply *must* take some pictures while you're in town. Nothing quite like New England in the fall!"

Staring at a brochure advertising the falls, which the town was apparently named for, a solution came to her. Later, when she was sleeping safely in a secured room, she'd forgive herself for the little white lie. "That's why I'm in town, actually." The gleam of the top magazine caught her attention, and Sky picked it up. "I'm working, writing an article—"

"I should've known!" The woman's eyes lit up behind her slipping reading glasses, her hands clapping together. "Do you write for one of those magazines?" Her bob of gray hair nodded toward *Travel Often.*

Sky was about to say no, but if she didn't find a way to procure a room at least until morning, she'd be sleeping on a park bench in a strange Vermont town. In October. "We rarely say so, but—I do, actually."

"You must've come to write about the harvest festival! Or..." The woman took in a deep breath as she flattened a hand over her chest. "Maybe one of our town's attractions?" Her energetic air at such a late hour amazed Sky, causing her to smother a yawn.

Her mind whirling, Sky almost blurted, "I'm writing an article about the Sleepy Inn," but somehow she thought that lie would haunt her all the way back to Omaha.

"Why, yes, I am." A glance at the brochure on top grabbed her attention. *Darcy's. The most unique rare book and antique map shop in New England.* Her pounding heart calmed, and the lie slipped out. "I'm writing an article about Darcy's." Her breathing was easier as she held up the declined Visa. "This is my travel card. Must be a glitch. I'll call in the morning, get this figured out. I'm sure it's all a misunderstanding."

"You'll want to catch Carter tomorrow morning, before he gets tied up with the festival," the woman added with a warm smile. Unlocking a case, she withdrew an iron key for Room Eight. "Darcy's opens at seven o'clock, but I suspect you knew that."

"Yep, sure did." Lying had never been something Sky enjoyed, but given the alternatives, she didn't see another feasible option.

She followed the woman up a staircase that wound around the wall, and spotted a grand fireplace in the adjacent corner.

"We serve breakfast, too, but you'll want to try one of Lucy's famous scones," the woman offered over her shoulder. "People drive all the way from

Burlington for them. Wednesday mornings, she serves chive and cheddar."

On cue, Sky's stomach rumbled. She hadn't eaten since that last gas station hot dog. One thing Colleen's cousins did not enjoy was eating in restaurants. *Stupid card worked then.* "I'm looking forward to trying them."

"Oh my, yes."

Sky would've given her last twenty-dollar bill to snuggle into bed with a rerun of *Friends*, but when the woman pushed open the door for her, she immediately noticed that the tiny room lacked a TV. She should've kept her mouth shut, been grateful that her ridiculous little lie obtained her a warm bed for a night, but...

"No cable?"

"No, dear. But there is a lovely little Juliet balcony in this room. Faces the sunrise." She waited for Sky to set her suitcase on the bed. "Need a wake-up call?"

"No, thank you."

"Get some rest. Carter Jensen, well, he can be a little exhausting. But I promise, he has a kind heart. Not a person in town who doesn't think so."

"Noted."

"Good night, dear." Before the door closed, the woman popped her head back in. "I'm Lisa. Lisa Bleeker. Feel free to use me in your article if it'll help."

Sky nodded. "Lisa." When Lisa didn't move, Sky reached for her notebook and scribbled down the name. "Bleeker."

"That's with two Es and no A."

"Got it."

The door clicked shut, and Sky dropped onto the bed. Yawns attacked her, one after another, until moisture ran down her cheeks.

It'd been a long day. *Long four days.* But Sky couldn't complain that she'd managed to escape the wedding disaster and army of hungry reporters eager to locate the woman who allegedly sabotaged such a perfect political match.

Someday, maybe ten years from now, she and Elaine would laugh about the debacle over coffee.

*Someday.*

But as it stood now, the story was all over the Internet, along with Sky's horror-struck expression when the bride *caught* her with the groom. Never mind that the palm on his chest was pushing him away. The media didn't care. And Elaine had *not* been able to keep the wedding from being canceled.

The best thing Sky could do for her sister's business and her own pride was to lay low for a while. Eventually she'd have to face Elaine. Until then, Sky only hoped she could keep from getting the boot at the Sleepy Inn, here in little Monroe Falls.

## CHAPTER 3

# Carter

"Moose!" Carter Jensen's coonhound stood on the edge of the boat dock, face and droopy ears a couple inches shy of the Arrow river.

This had happened before. Moose would wander off while Carter checked his emails and finished his first cup of coffee. The dog was notorious for finding stray brook trout swimming around the dock. Most times, Moose just fell in and the fish got away. Enough times, actually, for Carter to wonder if it was the same fish.

"Moose, let's go!" he called again as the dog leaned closer to the water. "You fall in, you have to stay home. Lucy'll kill you if you get her floors wet."

The coonhound debated a moment longer before reluctantly leaving the fish behind for another day. Moose trotted toward the truck.

Carter had spent a little extra time at his computer this morning, on an email about a Pennsylvania map from July 1863. He had a buyer on his short list for Civil War maps. If they had anything to do with Gettysburg, it was a sure sale. But his correspondence with the seller had him running behind this morning. He'd have to hope his cousin Lucy was willing to make a trip to Delaware by the end of the month to pick it up.

Moose jumped up onto the passenger seat in a single, slightly awkward pounce. Carter slammed the door and rounded the front of his old red Ford. He could hear his mom's lecturing voice telling him, *Trade it in. Get a newer model.* But Maggie had loved this old beater. He'd no sooner trade it in than give up fishing.

The truck bounced along the gravel road as Carter eased into Monroe Falls' city limits. The sun was slicing through branches, illuminating the leaves, some entangled overhead in the colors of ripe pumpkins.

Moose sat erect in his seat, his gaze scanning for squirrels. At his first sighting, he started grumbling under his breath. Before they hit the stop sign at the corner of Bleeker and Main, Moose had his head straight up in the air, nose pointed to the ceiling as he let out his doggy protests. *They're preparing for winter, Dad!*

Carter liked the town best at this early hour, when most of it was still asleep, when the only stirring was his dog in the passenger seat. Before the bustle of shop owners arrived to open their doors. Before the gaggle of fall tourists flooded the streets. Before Darcy's filled with the Hens.

Maggie had loved it all. But Carter, he cherished the silence.

A few sleepy blocks later, Carter and Moose slipped in through Darcy's side door. The aroma of Lucy's famous scones greeted him like a siren luring him in. It'd be fifteen minutes before any were ready, but his cousin would bring him one upstairs.

Moose bounded up the wide wooden staircase where his favorite bone waited. Carter followed him to his office, happy to successfully avoid an onslaught of chatty customers despite this morning's delay.

"You could at least pretend to like the customers," Lucy scolded, startling him as he unlocked the heavy wooden office door.

Pushing it open, Carter threw over his shoulder, "That's why I have you."

"Carter—"

"You brought me two," he interrupted, taking the plate from her. The ceramic instantly warmed his chilled hands.

"Of course I— Don't go changing the subject on me." She followed him to his humble desk.

"And what subject would that be?"

The old wooden table hardly appeared sturdy enough to support a cup of coffee, but he'd reinforced the worn legs. He liked things that way, with history.

He set his laptop on the table, but failed to open it. He planned to spend the entire morning with his latest treasure—a map of Vermont from their founding year. This one he'd not be selling, but adding to his own private collection. Some he displayed in the room across the hall, aptly labeled "Ahab's Cupboard," but most hung on the walls at home.

"Carter, it's harvest festival weekend. You can't just hide—"

"Watch me." He took a giant bite of scone, removing his heavy leather jacket as he savored the flaky, cheesy flavor. Delicious, as always. "Maybe bring me one more before you sell out?"

Lucy spun around at the door. "If you want another scone, you'll have to come down and get it yourself." With that, she flew away, the creak of the stairs fading one by one.

Opening Darcy's had been his cousin's idea, though she wouldn't let anyone give her credit for it. Moose sat obediently at Carter's feet, head tilted in expectation. "Too bad I never taught you how to fetch," Carter muttered as he tossed the dog a corner of his scone. Moose swallowed it whole, tail thumping against the hardwood floor as he waited for more.

Carter wasn't one for socializing, and when he did, he could only hold out for a short while before the task overwhelmed him. That was why he and Maggie had been so perfect together. Maggie had been social enough for both of them.

He scooped up the last bite of his first scone and stuffed it in. At the first chirps of customers downstairs, he donned his special cotton gloves and shoved away thoughts of the past. It still seemed unreal that his high school sweetheart—his wife—had been dead for almost seven years.

## CHAPTER 4

Sky

The side of her right foot ached, making Sky regret choosing her gray heeled boots, even if they did match her wrapped scarf. She'd only been thinking of making a good first impression on Darcy's owner. That the Sleepy Inn was half a dozen hilly blocks away unfortunately hadn't factored into her footwear decision.

In the distance, the sun fought to escape the billowing gray clouds. Sky adjusted the strap on her leather satchel as she crossed the narrow street, using the pinch of her elbow to keep out a light drizzle.

Sky had taken hundreds, probably thousands, of photographs in the past several years. Some had been of people, some nature, and some were even unique homes and shops. Despite that, she'd never been more than a tourist or a hobby photographer. Yet she was certain she could pull this off. Just one day to interview the shop's owner, take a few shots, and she could claim to spend the rest of her long weekend polishing that hypothetical article.

Rounding the final corner, Darcy's came into view, the two-story giant boasting a covered porch, white paneling, and fall foliage scattered before it. Someone Sky assumed was a customer rocked in a wooden chair on the porch, book clutched in hand. With its Victorian charm, the bookstore-café combination looked as though it *did* belong on a magazine cover. *How fitting.*

Sky stopped abruptly across the street, the heel of her boot catching on a sidewalk crack. Once she righted herself, she slipped her camera from the satchel and adjusted the lens until it perfectly captured the leaves' coppery hues. Framing the porch, she zoomed in to showcase that contented reader and snapped six extra shots.

She had dabbled with photography since high school, but it was a happy accident that she'd signed up for a photography course in college. She'd never gone anywhere since without a camera in hand.

Crossing the street, she approached, snapping more pictures with each step closer. She felt an odd sense of accomplishment as she flipped through the photos on the small screen on the camera's back. *Yes, this weekend might be exactly what I need.*

The long, white-painted wood stairs creaked beneath the weight of her boots. The reader in the chair, an older woman with silvering hair curled in at her chin and a fishing hat casting shadows over her eyes, failed to look up.

Behind the French doors' paneled windows, Sky caught the quick whir of a woman delivering a tray and remembered why she was here.

*A quaint, new-and-used bookstore that doubles as a café from morning until early afternoon,* according to the brochure. She'd read that not less than nine times this morning, gleaning tidbits like the makeup of those French doors: *alder wood.* The owner: *Carter Jensen.* And his specialty: *renowned for locating rare books and antique maps.*

"People don't just come from all over the country, they even cross oceans to get their hands on a treasure Carter hunts down for them," Lisa "Two Es and No A" Bleeker had told her that morning. She'd found Sky swiping an apple from the kitchen, and offered her a napkin. "He has a special gift for finding rare items."

Sleigh bells announced her arrival inside the café, drawing the attention of many, including the barista, whose chocolate-brown hair was tied up in a messy bun. *That's who I saw whisking by.* A gaggle of ladies looked up from their table, each in a mismatched chair, their conversation momentarily halted.

"You must be the travel writer." The waitress set her tray on the wooden counter, one that looked as if it'd been built from old barn wood. She extended a hand. "I'm Lucy."

"How did—"

Lucy shrugged. "Small town. Lisa called, gave us some warning. We didn't know any travel magazine was interested in featuring Darcy's."

"I thought for sure someone from the magazine would've called last week," Sky said, wondering who would be responsible for calling a business about being featured in a magazine. There must be a name for that position. *An editor? Public relations manager?* Sky pasted on a smile. "If this is a bad time—"

"It's always a bad time for Carter," Lucy mumbled, her eyes cast on the floor. "I'll check with him and see if he has any time today. In the meantime, I can fix you a cup, if you like?"

Sky was trying to cut back on her coffee addiction, but who was she kidding? Crossing the threshold of a place like this practically mandated one to have a cup of something. Preferably something that tasted like pumpkin. "I'd love something to drink. And one of your famous scones, if there are any left?"

"Scones'll be about ten minutes," Lucy said.

"You only writing about Darcy's? There's a whole festival weekend planned. Parade and bonfire tomorrow, homecoming game on Friday."

Sky was having a hard time listening to any actual words. The scent of well-thumbed books, aged pages, and brewing coffee nearly sent her into a trance. "I'll be including some of that in my article," she finally said, hoping to sound believable. "It helps to capture the town's essence."

"There's even a dance on Saturday," Lucy added, a twinkle in her eye as she carefully placed a white porcelain mug on the counter. "I hope you'll be staying in town for the weekend."

Taking her coffee, Sky sipped and smiled. "I wouldn't dream of missing it." She settled in at a small table near the window and pulled out her phone as Lucy disappeared into the kitchen. Still too early to call the bank.

Her phone was littered with texts, mostly from Elaine, of course. Some concerned, others full of empty threats that made Sky cringe. Her sister had every right to be upset, at least at Sky's hasty escape. But until Elaine calmed down and was willing to listen to reason, Sky couldn't deal with her. She'd do that after the weekend was over.

"Here you go, fresh from the oven!" Lucy slid a plate in front of Sky, shaking her from her troubled thoughts. "On the house," she added with a wink.

Sky shoved her phone back in her purse, failing

to read Elaine's half-dozen newer tirades. Today, she wouldn't think about the disaster wedding at all. "Why, thanks."

"I'll go see about Carter. He's upstairs, probably working on one of his old maps."

While Sky enjoyed her tasty chive and cheddar scone, she couldn't help but let her gaze wander the room. At least she'd remembered to pull out her notebook. But her attention was genuine—the rickety rotating wire bookracks full of worn paperbacks, the chalkboard behind the coffee counter beautifully spelling out today's scone-of-the-day. The way the sun glowed in the reflection of the worn, honey-hued hardwood floor.

She tossed the last flaky corner of her scone into her mouth and sank back into her rickety wooden chair in satisfaction. Once her card was unfrozen, she planned to order a dozen. *So tasty.* She played at taking notes, all the while thinking, *If there are any left after their morning rush thins out.* If they were as famous as Lisa claimed, there wouldn't be.

Lucy appeared at her table, an apologetic expression lingering in her eyes. "I'm sorry, but Carter asks that you come back later. He's in the middle of an important project. If you'd made an appointment—"

"It's no problem." Sky scooted out from her chair, brushing a couple of stray crumbs from her gray scarf. "What time's better?"

"Eleven?"

"Perfect. Eleven it is."

Though the delay was a little disappointing, she decided she'd roam the quaint little town and snap some photos. Couldn't hurt to look the part, after all. Sky waved good-bye with her notebook still in hand.

At the door, she hesitated. Lucy had busied herself behind the counter, leaving Sky with limited guilt about snapping a few impromptu pictures. It seemed a shame not to capture the essence of such a charming place, real article or fake.

Lowering her camera, she caught a glimpse of a man hidden in the shadowy stairwell, three steps from the main floor. *Carter?* His intense eyes scanned the café, then landed on Sky but quickly continued their quest to the kitchen. In a flash, the broad-shouldered man with a fresh day or two of stubble in jeans traveled from the staircase to the kitchen. Her stomach did a funny flip at the sight.

Her cheeks heated as she realized the gaggle of older women were staring at her curiously. Sky slipped out the door and hurried down the street as quickly as her heeled boots would take her.

arter

Carter held his breath as he leaned over the spacious table, a soft eraser in his gloved hand. He'd come across the antique map by chance, or *luck*, as many chose to believe. But Carter didn't. Luck had gotten him nowhere.

Though his cotton gloves promised to keep the oils from his hands off the parchment, he knew one could never be too careful. He gently erased a faint pencil mark at the top left corner and read, "1791 Vermont," mindful of its delicate parchment. He'd been searching for months to find a map of his home state to add to his collection. That this one was printed in its founding year—

"Carter, you've been working on that old map all morning." Lucy stood in the doorway, hands folded across her chest. "You need some fresh air."

"I'm taking Moose fishing later." At the mention of his name, the coonhound, formerly passed out beneath the table, lifted his head. His heavy brown ears flapped against the hardwood. "I need to get this framed first."

Lucy, shoulder leaning into the doorframe, pushed off the wall. "Your reporter's back."

He needed this last calm day to himself. The harvest festival would chew up enough of his time. Demand he be more social than he liked. And tonight, he needed to fix his great aunt's siding. That last windy storm had not so gently removed some of it from the left side of her house.

Carter straightened, stretching out a crick his neck. He could frame the map tomorrow if he got it under glass today. "Let her take some pictures around the place, then." He reached for the glass pane. "I'll talk to her tomorrow."

"It might do you some good to get out."

Once the glass was in place, he assessed his cousin's expression. "Oh, no. No, no, no."

"She's in town for the festival and needs someone to show—"

"*Lucy*." A warning hung in his tone.

She came around the table, placed a soft but firm

hand on his forearm. "Maggie's been gone seven years, Carter."

Hearing his late wife's name always made Carter feel as if someone was squeezing his heart. As though it might just turn to ash from clenched fingers. The passing years hadn't made life without Maggie any easier. If only he'd been home that awful weekend. If only he'd been here. *I might've had some clue.*

"She'd want you to be happy."

"I am."

"Brooding isn't happy." Lucy dropped her hand. "Besides, Darcy's could really use the publicity. Think of all the new customers it could draw into the café. They're national, you know." She took a step closer to the window, and turned back to him. "Think of the clients it could bring you."

Carter reached for his heavy leather jacket on the coat rack behind him. This room, also known as "Corps of Discovery" and once the old study, was the closest thing he had to an office here at Darcy's. Even if he didn't have an actual desk, at least he had a coat rack. Which made it feel official somehow. "Tell her to come back—"

A knock interrupted that. Carter spun around without thinking.

"I know I'm early."

Her chocolate eyes peeked over a Darcy's cup held to her lips. Carter tried responding, but found his mouth suddenly dry. His tongue stuck. In the doorway stood someone he hadn't expected. Her long hair fell across her shoulders, covering a gray scarf. The same woman he'd caught snapping pictures that morning.

"Carter'd like you to come back tomorrow," Lucy interjected. "He has to take his dog fishing."

The reporter's lips curled into a warm smile. "Lucky dog." Moose hopped up from his spot beneath the table, tail wagging in approval.

"She's kidding," Carter finally managed, despite his shock at her carefree response. Her outward appearance screamed *city*. "I was just about to run out for some lunch."

"You don't eat at the café?"

"Not today," Carter answered. "I have to meet a client at Wild Jack's in a couple of hours. Thought I'd grab some lunch there. Why don't you join me, bring your questions along?" He could've picked Lucy's jaw up off the floor with the tip of his boot.

"Perfect." Her eyes traveled between him and Lucy. "I'll just snap a few pictures until you're ready to go." She turned and surprisingly, Moose followed.

Carter caught his chest heaving as if he'd sprinted up the stairs. It took a moment of deep, controlled breaths to slow his breathing. "Don't get any ideas, Lucy."

ky

Earlier, Sky sat on a park bench in pitiful tears, the last of the pumpkin gone from her taste buds, preparing a list of questions for her interview with Carter Jensen. She had to do something to keep her mind off her dilemma. The bank claimed she called in yesterday, cancelled her card, and froze her accounts. A new card was in the mail, but it would do her no good here in Vermont.

"Thanks, Elaine," she muttered, certain her sister was behind this. Probably some form of payback for not answering those most recent texts. Elaine surely expected Sky to call her now that she had no money and beg for her help.

She returned to Darcy's with dried eyes and roamed the upstairs, surprised to realize they'd mostly left the walls intact. Something good to ask about. Her hasty inn room research had shown that until about six years ago, Darcy's had been a six-bedroom family home. *In the Mills family for generations,* she jotted.

She took her time passing closed doors on either side of the hall, Moose at her side, as she read the engraved plaques that labeled the rooms: "Ahab's Cupboard," "Huck's Hideaway," "Nobert's Nook."

At the end of the hallway, a beautiful sign etched in a piece of driftwood hung on the arched beam announcing "Lizzie's Loft." The majority of the book-covered walls were here, in a mixture of new and old shelving, Sky noted.

She snapped a few photos, adjusting her lighting between the dim hallway and the well-lit, sunny loft with cushioned chairs propped in odd corners and mismatched footrests. With the skylights, the lighting for reading was best in this open room.

For a moment, she almost believed she was a travel writer. A sinking sensation bit at the corners of her heart, but she pushed them away. Sky had to keep her mind on the positive. Like how the corridor of rooms, all labeled, piqued her interest.

She smiled, remembering Carter in "Corps of Discovery." That the room was filled with maps was no surprise. She added another question to her list. It might be an easy icebreaker topic for a lunch date that already had her stomach in twists. *Not a date.*

Moose snuck a silky ear under her hand, and huffed a friendly, *uff!*

"Ready to go?" Carter asked from the hallway opening.

Sky's heart pounded, but only because she needed Carter to believe she was a reporter. It had nothing to do with those blue eyes, somehow bluer in the dimly lit hallway. "Yep." She trailed after him down the stairs, trying hard to keep up with his long strides as he practically raced through the front of Darcy's and out the door.

"Is hell freezing over?"

Sky nearly collided into Carter's back as he jolted to a stop and spun toward the same woman still in the rocking chair.

"Really funny, Mom."

"You never use the front door."

"Isn't it time for you to get back to work?"

"Your mom works for you?" Sky asked without thinking. Then she bit her lip. Had she done her homework, she probably would've known such a detail.

"Work's a loose term," Carter tossed over his shoulder, his eyes never leaving the woman rocking in the chair. "Mom, this is a reporter from—" Carter turned to Sky and asked, "What magazine did you say?"

"Travel—"

"One of those," Carter said, unimpressed. As if she was wasting his time. Though she'd never really interviewed anyone outside of engaged couples planning their special day, Sky couldn't understand his disinterest. Shouldn't he want to gain exposure for his business? If it were a legit article, anyway.

"Where you headed?"

"Wild Jack's. Have to meet a client." Quickly, Carter patted his mom's shoulder before hurrying down the steps to the sidewalk. Sky was forced to chase after him, and didn't catch up until they reached the street.

*Guess we're walking.*

"Your mom seems like a lovely woman," Sky said, because she felt she needed to say something.

Carter's shoulders shook with a silent laugh. "Yeah."

"Are you close?"

Shoving his hands in his jacket pockets, he raised an eyebrow at her. "What kind of article are you writing, exactly?"

"A good one." When he failed to smile, she went on. "I'm not planning to write about your relationship with your mom. I was just curious."

"She's my mom. Why wouldn't we be close?"

Sky should drop it, but she couldn't help herself. "It's just the way you two were arguing—"

"Banter."

"What?"

"We don't argue. My mom. Me. It's never anything more than good-hearted banter."

"Ah."

"Don't you banter with your mom?"

"She passed away before my vocabulary had more than ten words." That statement stopped Carter in his tracks, and Sky nearly slammed into him again. "You've got to stop doing that," she chided. "I don't know how many times I can survive running into a brick wall."

"I'm sorry."

"Just keep your feet moving. I think we'll be okay."

"I meant about your mom. I didn't mean to be insensitive or anything."

Sky smiled, oddly comforted by this small gesture. Compassion toward a complete stranger.

*arter*

This woman asked too many questions for Carter's liking, but he certainly didn't mind watching her lips move. Couldn't seem to keep his eyes from drawing back to them. Which only complicated things.

He interrupted some question about "Norbert's Nook" he didn't feel like explaining. "Where did you say you were from?"

"Nebraska."

He raised an eyebrow. "I didn't take you for Midwest girl." He nodded at her attire. The fashionable faux leather jacket, the perfectly layered scarf.

"Born and raised." Sky twirled her straw in her water glass, her eyes failing to lift from the rim.

He reached for his iced tea and took a long sip. Feeling guilty that his unfair assessment had thrown her into an awkward silence, he added, "I've been to Nebraska."

"It's a popular place." The mocking twinkle to her eyes put him at ease. "Did you go to pick up a map?"

The server appeared at their table, slipping a pad from her apron. "Ready to order now?"

Carter nodded at Sky.

"I'm okay with just the water, thanks."

The way her troubled eyes studied her straw roused Carter. "We'll take two Monster Burger baskets with fries."

"But—"

"Thanks."

"I can't—I mean, I'm not that hun—"

"You can't leave town without trying one of Jack's famous Monster Burgers." Carter helped himself to more iced tea, deciding to change the subject. "Round out your article nicely. As for Nebraska, I went on a fishing trip. Years ago. A place kind of in the southwest, if I remember right. Medicine Creek?"

Sky's eyes ignited with a sparkle he hadn't seen since he first spotted her in the doorway of his study. "Medicine Creek? It's—"

The light dimmed almost as quickly as it had appeared, which only stirred something uneasy in the pit of his stomach. Not the urge to bring back the light, no. But something. "Yes?"

Their server reappeared, sliding two baskets and a plastic squeeze bottle of ketchup in front of them.

Carter blinked. "That was fast."

"Jack must've known you were coming. I'll be back to check on you in a little bit. Enjoy."

"It's a nice spot." Sky squirted a blob of ketchup in the side of her basket. "Just surprised you've heard of it, that's all." She dunked a fry, but before taking a bite, asked, "Do you take a lot of fishing trips?"

"Used to." He cleared his throat, but when that failed, he reached for his iced tea and drained it down to the half-melted ice cubes. He couldn't talk about this. Not today. Fishing trips outside his river were a thing of the past. A haunting memory of the failure he'd been. That day Maggie needed him most. "But now I have a business to run, you know. Easier to stay close to home."

The straight line in those curvy lips warned him she wasn't satisfied with his answer, so Carter tried changing the subject. "You staying in town all weekend?" He nodded to her notebook. "There's a lot going on you could put in your article. Maybe enough for two."

"Mrs. Bleeker gave me a schedule. Uh ... Lisa." Sky pulled a teal-blue flyer from her purse and waggled it. "Sounds like a parade, bonfire, homecoming, opening of a time capsule."

"You're forgetting the pancake feed." He pointed his glass at her, forgetting until he went to take a drink that he'd emptied it. "It's no fake maple syrup on those pancakes, you know."

At Sky's smile, he felt his shoulders drop. If they could keep the questions light, he might just survive this lunch. But he knew it was too much to hope for. Darcy's partially became what it was in Maggie's memory. At Sky's next question, he had no choice but to tell her the truth.

"Let me get a refill first." Carter waved his empty glass, waiting for their waitress to grab a full pitcher of tea from the counter. Sky seemed preoccupied, fidgeting with her phone. Her eyebrows drew together and her eyes fell shut. The slow rise and fall of her shoulders reminded him of someone counting to ten to calm themselves. "Everything all right?"

"Yep." She shoved the phone back in her purse. "Just my ... editor. Deadlines and things."

Carter didn't believe it, but their server cut him off before he had a chance to press. "If you two need anything else, let me know."

"I'm meeting a Kyle Jacobs here at noon," Carter told her. "If he comes in, seat him and get him a beer, will you?"

"Of course."

"So, back to my question," Sky finally said, most everything in the basket dealt with. Her wrist rested on her notepad, pen teetering between two fingers in a frenzy. "How'd you decide to name your store Darcy's?"

After a deep breath, Carter plunged in to a question that shouldn't haunt him anymore. "A tribute to my late wife Maggie." Oddly, his voice didn't crack at the mention of her name. He couldn't remember a time in the last seven years that it hadn't. So, he pushed on while he could. "She loved Jane Austen. Even started a book club called 'Darcy's Ladies.' She passed away, seven years ago. Unexpectedly."

He hadn't realized he'd been staring at the table until a soft hand covered his. "I'm so sorry, Carter."

When he met her eyes, understanding lingered there. They'd talked too much about death today.

He couldn't help but glance at her left hand, still outstretched on the table, though she'd retracted the contact. *No ring.* "'Lizzie's Loft,' that's a tribute to Elizabeth Bennett. I never read those books, you see, but my cousin helped come up with clever names. In Maggie's honor."

"Lucy?"

"Yeah. She's been great. I couldn't have done any of it without her." What would life be if Lucy hadn't been at his side, insisting this business would give him purpose again? "My name's on the paperwork, but don't let that fool you. She keeps Darcy's running."

"Her scones aren't half bad, either."

"Half—" But then he met her eyes and caught

the twinkle. *Mischievous.* "I'll have you know folks come clear from Burlington for those."

"Special ingredient?" She poised her pen.

Carter shrugged. "Magic."

"Magic?"

"If there's a special ingredient, you can rest assured my cousin hasn't left that secret with me." Carter mourned the beeping of his watch that warned him their lunch was nearly over. He shut it off. "My client'll be here soon."

"Why here?" Sky asked. "Why meet at Wild Jack's and not Darcy's if you're discussing business?"

"We don't serve alcohol."

Sky's laughter filled an emptiness Carter hadn't realized existed. Those lips formed the most beautiful smile. He wanted to trace them with his finger. What was coming over him? He didn't even know this woman sitting across from him.

"You make a valid point," said Sky.

He spotted a tall man who filled the doorway. Boots, a mop of dark hair, and a belt buckle the size of a dessert plate. Jamie nodded at Carter as she seated him in a booth near the window, just far enough away that he could discreetly finish his lunch with Sky without feeling too rude.

"That your client?"

"Mm-hmm." He hoped she had more questions, if only to have an excuse to see her again. He gambled and asked, "If you were planning to take in the parade tomorrow, you could come with me." It sounded lame the moment the words left his lips. The parade wasn't exactly an extravagant event. It only spanned the few blocks of Main Street and would be over within an hour. From the inn, Sky could make it there in minutes on foot. Surely, she didn't need a tour guide, but it was the soonest he'd have free time again. "It'd give you a chance to ask more of your questions."

"Questions, yes. Yes. Okay." She replaced her notebook in her bag. "Meet you at Darcy's tomorrow?" Then she smiled.

He told himself the rapid beating of his heart had nothing to do with the beautiful woman sitting across from him. *Nothing at all.* Especially not the sound of her laughter already embedded in his memory.

"Two o'clock."

ky

Sky shouldn't have turned on her phone. She'd nearly blown her cover in Wild Jacks when she saw the latest text message she'd received.

**Elaine**: **YOU CAN'T HIDE FOREVER. I WILL FIND YOU, SKYLAR!**

Sky found a bench two blocks shy of the Sleepy Inn and plopped down to reread the message. Just to be certain she wasn't overreacting.

"Nope."

Elaine loved her, Sky knew she did. She'd looked out for Sky all her life, first when their mom passed, and then when their dad did too. She'd given Sky her first meaningful job at Catching the Bouquet, which Elaine had started on her own and built into a small empire.

Guilt only churned at that thought.

The Gilbertson/Stovermeyer wedding was to be their biggest event to date, not only in terms of profit, but in the potential future clients it would bring. Between the two political powerhouse families, they knew everyone. And Elaine had handed Sky the most responsibility she'd ever been given: total charge of Ken. The groom. The governor's nephew.

For a fleeting moment, she wondered what it might be like to live in a quiet little New England town like Monroe Falls. To slow down in life and see what she'd been missing amidst the hustle. She released a groaning sigh and sank back on the bench. What would it be like to plan smaller, country weddings for people who didn't care about votes?

*Or to not plan any at all?*

The thought both shocked and soothed. It was a crazy notion. Move halfway across the country. Start over. The story was leaked all over the Internet. Last night, she caught her first glimpse of a photo of her falling out a second story window, a silver heel flying, barely missing a robin.

To keep from breaking down, Sky called her best friend.

In the middle of the second ring, Colleen's sharp tone snapped, "Why on earth is your phone on!"

"Hi, Coll." Sky took a deep breath and sagged further into the wooden bench.

"Are you *trying* to give your sister GPS coordinates?"

"If she planned to hunt me down, you know she would've done that already. I think she's trying to teach me a lesson." At least the day was turning out to be nice, as the drizzle had given way to a tiny bit of sunshine. "But Elaine *did* cancel my card. I can't even pay for my room!"

"Honey!" Colleen's sharp tone changed to motherly in that single word. "Why didn't you call me sooner? I'll wire you some funds. Or just call, I can read them my card number."

"Coll—"

"Don't worry about it. You can pay me back later."

For the first time since she fled, Sky felt a wave of relief.

She'd been on pins and needles during the entire car ride with Laney and Deke. She didn't have the heart to tell Colleen that her cousin had gone out of her way to remind Sky how *lucky* she was that they agreed to smuggle her out of town. Laney'd peppered her with the most uncomfortable questions, despite the disapproving looks of her reserved hubby.

"The town's nice," Sky said finally. "Charming, actually."

"Can't beat New England in the fall."

"Maybe I should move here," Sky mumbled under her breath. It sure beat the city's bustle. She'd forgotten how much she enjoyed the slower pace of a small town. How enjoyable she found the quiet. Cars sputtered up the intersecting roads as Colleen commiserated in Sky's ear. A couple met at a four-way stop, the hum of their conversation traveling to her.

"You know, Sky, I've heard crazier ideas."

"No," she said immediately. "I'm not moving to Vermont. That's ridiculous, Colleen. I mean, what would I do without you?" The temptation to start over somewhere was already crawling toward her. Self-talk was Sky's only defense. "It's just fear, right? Because I'm afraid to face everyone back home. I can't *really* live here."

"Skylar, darling, if you think you could move to the moon and avoid *me*, you're wrong. I'd hunt you down no matter where you ventured off to. Count on me to force my loving friendship on you."

It was so good to hear her best friend's voice. She almost said as much, but she didn't want Colleen to know how out of sorts she'd been. Not after all the trouble she'd gone through to help Sky escape. "How bad was it?"

Colleen sputtered a laugh. "It was a disaster. One for the books, that's for sure. The press is eating this up. Better that you left or they'd be hounding you day and night for an exclusive."

Sky, shoulders slumping, looked up into the trees, admitting, "I should've figured it out sooner. *Kenny* was a piece of work. He's been hitting on me since the cake tasting."

"You were a pawn in their little childish games. Don't beat yourself up. She didn't want to marry him either. We've both known that since the dress fitting. It was an arranged marriage for political gain."

"You think so?"

"I mean, she practically said as much. Doesn't take a genius to read between the lines."

"You don't think I should come back now, help Elaine with damage control?"

"Don't be fooled, Sky. Your sister's frazzled, for sure. But if there's one thing we can both commend her on, it's how she handles herself during a crisis. Give her time to cool off. Just be careful not to lash out," Colleen warned. "She might report you as kidnapped."

Sky could just imagine the horror if the authorities had burst into Wild Jack's earlier and *rescued* her from lunch with Carter. Her skin tingled at the memory of his touch when she placed her hand on his. *Carter.* What would he think about all this? Hopefully, he'd never have to find out the truth. Or Lucy, either. Or Mrs. Bleeker at the Sleepy Inn.

"You're not sleeping on a park bench, are you?" Colleen asked.

"No." Sky laughed then, because what else could she do? Then she entertained Colleen with the travel writing tale, careful to watch for eavesdroppers. But the side street remained sleepy throughout most of her retelling. Moose and all.

"You can't write to save your life."

"I know. It's such a disaster."

"Well, not everything sounds hopeless. Tell me more about the hunk who runs the bookstore. He sounds positively dreamy."

arter

Carter spent his morning fishing. He'd hear about it soon enough, when Lucy caught him sneaking in the back door. He had a client coming tomorrow morning to view a map of Maryland from 1805 and it wasn't framed yet, but for now, he'd sit in his boat and enjoy the quiet. All except for Moose sleep-growling and kicking at the worn vinyl of the cushioned bench.

But Carter didn't mind the dog's company. The fish weren't biting anyway. He just couldn't take Lucy's inquiry about his lunch with Sky.

Or Sky, for that matter.

Why'd he offer to take her to the parade? It'd been impulsive, and he knew better than to act on impulse. It'd never gotten him anything but disappointed.

The fishing trip that took him away from Maggie during her last days on earth was an impulse. The trip to Montana to fish with his college roommate when his little sister was killed in a car accident a decade ago was on a whim. The trip to Delaware to see his old high school buddy had taken him out of town when his mother's dear friend Molly had fallen and broken her hip. Impulse after impulse. What had they brought Carter of any worth?

He pushed open the cooler with his foot, wishing it were late enough in the day for a beer, but settling instead for a grape-flavored sports drink.

Not a day had gone by since Maggie's passing that he hadn't thought of her. The sting had eased, but not the guilt he carried about his absence when she needed him most. And now... now he was thinking about another woman. One he *just* met.

"What am I doing?" he muttered to Moose, shifting enough in his seat to rock the boat. Carter's rough motion threw Moose off the bench, but the dog just grumbled and readjusted. He couldn't help but laugh as the coonhound reoriented himself into reality. "Sorry, buddy, no squirrels here."

Moose had been a blessing. A gift from his mom

six months after Maggie passed. It'd been his first inkling of hope for returning to normal life. Or as normal a life as he could imagine.

*It's been seven years, Carter.*

Lucy's words echoed now, but he wasn't sure they were enough to alleviate the guilt at his thoughts about moving on. *Dating* a woman. Was it wrong to yearn for someone to sit with on his deck? Someone he could share the sunset with while eating grilled burgers and talking about their day.

*Wouldn't I just let her down, too?*

"Dang it," he muttered, embarrassed by his own thoughts. He caught Moose's attention in time to keep the dog from toppling into the water after a piece of floating greenery. "I'm turning into a woman."

Carter pulled in his line and decided to head back to Darcy's.

---

The parade had already started by the time Carter returned. He spent the better part of the morning dodging texts and phone calls, and instead finished the work on his great aunt's siding. Anything to avoid going into the center of town.

Until he heard Arthur was back in town.

The man who killed his little sister when he

crashed the car he was driving. The same man, though cleared of all guilt, who left town without so much as an apology and stayed cleared for a decade. The man who had hurt his cousin with his abrupt departure.

For the first couple of years after Abbie's death, Carter had been furious, eager to blame the man who fled. *If it hadn't been for Maggie...* One of the greatest things she ever did for Carter was help him let go of his anger. To forgive Arthur. To let Abbie's death be what it truly was—an accident.

*But Lucy...* His cousin had cared for Arthur, waited by his bedside while he was in the hospital. And the man left town for a decade.

"Carter, there you are!" Lucy blocked his path to the stairs. "I need you to deliver these scones to Mrs. Aberton by four. They're for her cat's birthday party. I would, but—"

He stared into her eyes, searching them for clues of her true feelings. "Are you okay with this? Are you okay with Arthur being *here?*"

"Carter..."

"Because if you're not—"

"I'm fine. I promise." Her locked gaze was the reassurance he needed to know his cousin could handle herself. He admired how strong Lucy was, how she managed to push forward no matter what. "Sky's upstairs."

*Crap, Sky!* "If you need anything, Luce—"

"Go!"

Carter rushed past and bounded up the stairs, ignoring curious looks from the last remaining customers. Lucy should be locking up by now anyway. The entire town was expected to turn out.

He'd apologize for making her wait. For the plans he was about to cancel. Up the stairs, Carter steadied himself with a deep breath.

But the moment he caught her reading a book, Sky spun around. Wide brown eyes met his, like a child caught stealing a cookie before dinner. "I—I was just browsing." Her flushed cheeks and obvious embarrassment softened something inside of him.

Carter let out a deep belly laugh.

Sky, hand on her hip, eyebrow cocked, demanded, "What's so funny?"

Carter wasn't prepared for what that playful, challenging look would do to him. His heart thumped against his chest in slowly increasing beats as his eyes drew to those beautiful lips. What he wouldn't give for a kiss...

"Are we going to the parade?"

*Right. The parade.*

Carter hated the social aspect of it all. He had to admit it was a great way to see the community pull together, but that was always Maggie's thing. Social-izing. Right now, the idea of standing on a crowded street, sandwiched between people he knew too much about, suffocated him. "I've got an idea."

He surprised himself as his hand reached out, but he caught it and lowered it to his side.

But not in time for Sky's confused eyes not to spot the impulse. He turned abruptly, leaving her to put back the book and trail after him down the stairs.

 ky

Sky'd attended her fair share of parades. But they held an entirely different appeal from the top of this two-story brick building. Folding lawn chairs waited behind them; Carter had thought of everything. Even this high, it required her to lean forward, craning her neck over the ledge to see more than the crowd of people packed on the sidewalk across the street.

Though empty, this was one of three commercial buildings Carter's dad owned and leased, he'd explained, the only one that presently sat empty. Though they'd come in the back door, Sky caught a glimpse of empty rooms and its large storefront window. It was easy to imagine a small craft store or even a photography studio filling such a space.

"They do the parade every year," Carter explained, pulling a chair closer to the edge for her. "The different businesses, they sponsor floats. And our homecoming game's tomorrow, so the high school always has floats representing the Monroe Falls Mariners." Carter eased back in his chair, nonchalantly tucking himself a bit out of sight, Sky noted.

"Firetrucks, hay bales, a marching band. Horses, too?"

"The usual small town parade."

"You're not much for them?" Sky asked, her eyes traveling the few blocks that spanned Main Street. It was that or she'd be caught staring at him. She'd been drawn to him since the first time she spotted him in the shadows on the stairs and she didn't know what to do about. In a couple of days, she'd be gone.

"If you've seen one parade..." Carter shrugged.

The screech of hinges in desperate need of oiling rang out above the music below. They'd had to climb a fire escape ladder and through a hatch to get to the roof, and now someone else was following suit.

"That'll be my mom." Carter pushed out of his chair to help the woman. The *porch banterer* from Darcy's. She wore the same fishing hat, Sky noticed, but instead of her heavy jacket, it was a teal cotton T-shirt this time, layered with a long-sleeve white tee beneath.

At a loud boom from below, Sky leaned forward to investigate.

"Careful there." Carter's hand rested on her shoulder, encouraging her to sit back a little. "Don't want to tip the chair too far forward."

"Right." She tried to focus on the few people on the sidewalk across the street. Anything to distract her from the comforting heat of his touch. How long had it been since Sky had even been on a date? Catching the Bouquet kept her going nonstop. There hadn't been time for things like dating.

"It's mostly just floats," Carter added. Kids had their hands outstretched for flying candy. "But the town enjoys it."

"Charming place."

"The best." He glanced over his shoulder. "Better see to my mom quick."

It was easy in this moment to envision living in a town like this one. One where every business closed up early to support a parade.

Sky dug her camera out from her satchel and snapped a few pictures of unique floats. Even if the article were a figment, she needed a reminder that she could start over if she wanted. Maybe wedding planning wasn't in her future any longer, but she found herself less sad about that with each passing day.

She glanced at the pair, talking a few steps away from the edge. Easing back in her chair, she ignored the banter. Whether it was about her or something else, she didn't care.

"Is the parade boring you, dear?" Mrs. Jensen asked, taking the chair Carter had occupied earlier. He stood behind her, arms folded. He shrugged at Sky, offering a small smile in apology.

"Not at all!" Sky could feel the strain of her cheeks against the cheesy smile surely plastered on her face. "I love it, actually."

"Why the frown earlier?"

"I was just thinking, that's all."

"If it's the parade, it's okay to say so. It's not terribly exciting. Not like we have anyone twirling fire."

Sky laughed at that. "Those parades are overrated."

"I hear you're a travel writer. I'm Pam, by the way." She pointed a thumb over her shoulder. "This one calls me Mom, but I don't always claim him."

The twinkle in Pam's eyes warmed a spot in Sky's heart. One that hadn't been warmed in too long a time. Elaine was a wonderful sister, but she didn't have a lot of time for the small things. Like compassion. Or banter.

"She's my mom whether she wants to be or not," Carter interjected, that smile causing another part of Sky to stir.

"Your folks miss you?" Pam asked. "With you on the road so much?"

"Mom…" Warning hung in Carter's voice.

Sky hated lying about the travel writing, but she no longer knew how to set things right without finding herself on the streets. Until Colleen's wire came through, she didn't have any way back to Burlington should she need it, unless she walked. At least she could stick to the truth about this. "My parents aren't living."

"Sorry to hear that." Pam's gentle hand tapped Sky's and they shared a sad smile. "You still miss them." Not a question.

"Every day."

"Did they like to travel?"

The question caught Sky off guard, and for a moment she forgot the lie she'd spun. "Dad liked to go on fishing trips, actually. He said that was all the traveling he needed."

From the corner of her eye, Sky caught the smile fade from Carter's face and a frown chiseled in its place. "I forgot something at the store," he said, dropping his arms. "Sky, you okay to hang out with my mom until I get back?"

She had no chance to do more than nod before he shot away toward the hatch. His sudden departure left her feeling a little empty and a bit confused, something that must've shown on her face.

"Don't feel bad, honey." Pam leaned forward. "That one's the float with the homecoming court. I used to change diapers for half those kids," she commented. "Anyway, Carter blames himself. Not a thing any of us can say to convince him it wasn't his fault."

"Blames himself?"

Pam adjusted her hat, her hazel eyes falling on Sky's folded hands in her lap. "Maggie. Brain aneurism. Very sudden. No warning."

"His wife." Sky recalled from yesterday's interview. But of course Carter hadn't mentioned what happened. "I—I didn't know. That's so awful."

"Carter, he was away in Montana. On a fishing trip. Took two hours for us to get hold of him. Nothing he could've done, even if he'd been home. But you can't convince him of that, even all these years later. He's never been one to let people get too close. But since then, it's been even worse."

"Is that why Lucy does the traveling?" Sky asked. "To pick up the items he finds?"

"He's afraid to go any farther than Burlington. Won't admit it if you ask, but he hasn't been more than a two-hour drive from home since Maggie left us."

*arter*

Before he could dodge her, Carter spotted Mrs. Gentry darting toward him. She waved with the duffel bag she called a purse, calling out as she wove through the crowd of people gathering for the bonfire.

Lucy owed him. She forced that scone delivery on him. She owed him big time. If only she'd taken them to Mrs. Aberton herself, he'd never have seen the bonfire smoke rising from Fall Into Pumpkins.

"I haven't been to one of these in years!" Sky had said. "Lucy mentioned it earlier and it sounded wonderful. Can we go? Please?"

No saying *no* to that smile. But it was the sparkle

in Sky's soft brown eyes that convinced him to take her. He wasn't sure what they were doing, exactly. This couldn't go anywhere. But he was certainly enjoying Sky's company.

"Carter, there you are!" Mrs. Gentry reached out and squeezed his arm, just like back in second grade. "I wanted to tell you my mother *loved* that baroque angel. How ever did you find one hand-carved from marble?"

"Angel?" Sky repeated. The instant flush of red on her cheeks made Carter smile. He stretched his cheeks, uncertain why they ached so much today.

"Why yes, Carter can find anything. Even a nineteenth century marble angel from France."

"Mrs. Gentry," Carter said, realizing he'd not introduced the women. "This is Sky Emerson. She's a travel writer."

"Oh! A travel writer? Are you writing about Monroe Falls?"

"Darcy's," Sky said, shaking the extended hand. "But I'm considering expanding the article. Monroe Falls is really a charming town. I didn't realize Carter dealt in more than books and maps."

*Expanding the article?*

"You're in town during a great weekend. So many things you could write about." Mrs. Gentry adjusted her thick purse strap, shoving it higher up on her shoulder. "Have you been to the falls?"

Sky shook her head.

"You make sure Carter here takes you before you leave. Any article about Monroe Falls would be incomplete without a stop there."

"I'll be sure to see them before I go."

The words struck on odd chord *before I go.* Carter knew Sky had no plans to stay. She was only in town on an assignment. In a few days, she'd leave for the next one. Though he'd accepted all that already, he didn't much care for the slight sinking feeling in his stomach at the thought of never seeing that smile again.

When Mrs. Gentry was swallowed up by the crowd, Carter scanned the area for an unoccupied hay bale near the exit, pushing away unwanted thoughts. "I can save us seats, grab us some lemonade, if you want to take some pictures."

The light in Sky's eyes might've been the glimmer of setting sun, but Carter didn't think so. That eager look reminded him of Moose first alerting to a squirrel. He slipped through the crowd toward the table offering refreshments.

"Cute girl you got there." Cindy, one of Maggie's closest friends, handed over two cool cups and shoved a napkin with two sugar cookies shaped like pumpkins in the crook of his arm. "I didn't know you were dating again, Carter."

Guilt smacked him so hard he staggered back a step, the drinks sloshing over onto his hands, but he managed to save the cookies. "I'm not."

"Oh?"

"She's a travel writer. Writing an article on Darcy's. Monroe Falls," he corrected himself. "That's all."

Cindy's attention was stolen briefly by her daughter, a little girl in pigtails yanking on her apron. *April.* She'd just turned five a couple of weeks ago, if he'd heard his mom right. A friend's daughter Maggie was never able to meet. But the usual sting didn't carry its full bite.

"Carter, Maggie would want you to be happy. You know that."

"Thank you for the lemonade." He spun around, spilling more on his hand, but hurried away before Cindy could hand him another napkin. This was why he avoided big social gatherings such as this. Because reminders of Maggie were everywhere. And where those reminders were, there were also people telling him it was okay to move on.

He failed Maggie. How could he ever risk letting down someone else like that?

"Saw that jostling there. You have anything left in those cups?"

Sky's teasing voice shook him from his gloomy haze when he returned to her. She reached for the nearly smashed cookies and set them on the bale she'd claimed for them.

The setting sun made her dark chocolate hair

shimmer with a slight golden hue. "I might have tripped," he lied, taking a seat next to her.

"Here." Sky dug in her tote bag, producing a paper napkin. Her soft graze against his hand had him staring at her slender fingers. It'd been years since the thought of holding someone's hand even flashed through his mind.

"Where's Moose?" Sky asked, nodding toward a golden retriever a few yards away. "Is he not a fan of bonfires?"

"Probably passed out on my couch he's not allowed on. Took him fishing this morning." That made Sky smile as she raised the cup of lemonade to her lips. "Your dad liked to fish?" Carter asked, because he had to talk about some topic. Fishing seemed the safest of all his present choices.

"Yeah." Sky wrapped both hands around her Styrofoam cup. "Me, too." Carter noted her light-pink manicured nails and wondered again how a woman who looked so city could talk so easily about fishing. "He used to take me, when I was younger."

"But you don't fish anymore. Does anyone in your family like to fish?"

The outburst of laughter was unexpected. "If you gave my sister a fishing pole, she wouldn't even know what it was for." Sky took a sip of her lemonade, her smile growing. "I can't even imagine what she'd do with a worm, but I'd pay a lot of money to see it!"

"She sounds…" But Carter couldn't think of any way to sugar coat the truth.

"Delightful?" Mischievousness twinkled in Sky's eye. It brought a smile to his lips. "I love her. I promise I do. But there are certainly days I wonder how the two of us ended up in the same family." The smile faded as Sky's gaze became distant. "But she's family. I love her no matter what. It's a promise we made each other."

"Older sister?"

"Yeah."

He wanted to ask more but reminded himself she wasn't his date. She wasn't really even his friend. Just a travel writer passing through town who'd be gone by Monday.

Still, he didn't like the frown that had formed across her lips. Carter reached behind him for the cookies, hoping they'd make her smile, but found his hand meeting something furry instead. A goat leisurely chewed the remains of the napkin. Their eyes met, and they laughed together. As though it was the most natural thing in the world to be sitting on a hay bale together, enjoying this small moment.

"Guess we won't be getting any cookies." Sky reached out a hand to pat the goat behind the ears. He obliged her for a moment, then trotted off after his next treasure.

"Guess not."

As the dusky sky gave way to the first glittering

of stars, a pumpkin patch employee added a pallet to the fire. It roared to life, the heat flashing against the legs of his jeans. "When's the last time you went fishing?"

"Wow." Sky peered into her cup, then out at the fire. "Has to have been at least fifteen years."

Carter couldn't stop himself before the words were out. "I think it's time to change that."

What was happening? They had a date. To go fishing.

It occurred to Sky that she couldn't recall when she'd gone on her last date. She'd been so buried in planning weddings, agonizing over every detail to please not only their clients but her sister, that she'd left little time for things like dating. She'd given up after too many complaints about her lack of time.

To top things off, Colleen's wire hadn't come through. Some complication at the bank. Elaine could hold a grudge longer than anyone Sky knew, but she wasn't yet ready to call her sister.

"Honey, if I have to fly out there and hand-deliver a check, I will."

"But how am I supposed to pay for this room?" Sky moaned, looking around the well-appointed space. When the weekend was over, then she'd go back and make things right.

"I already took care of it."

Colleen. A godsend. Always had been, since second grade when Sky sat in a puddle of chocolate milk in her brand new white pants and Colleen tied her favorite rain jacket around Sky's waist to hide it.

"Thank you, Coll. I don't know what I'd do without you."

After a quick update on the home front—Elaine was still doing her best to do damage control with the media, including the shots of Sky falling out that window. It was only by luck the party bus pulled up and blocked the photographer's view of Laney's getaway car.

"On the plus side, Stovermeyer's not exactly getting a lot of sympathetic press or future voters. But they're still painting you the villain."

"Of course they are." They laughed at that. Sky dropped onto the blue and white quilt, thankful she'd have a bed to sleep in again tonight. She couldn't ask yet another favor, though she desperately wanted some advice on what to do about Carter Jensen.

"Have fun with this, Sky," Colleen said after a

long, easy silence. "You're a travel writer this weekend. Soak it up, take some great pictures. Hey, maybe write that article for kicks. Who knows? You might be good at it."

Sky doubted that. Her creativity didn't include words, only pictures.

Hours after she hung up, Sky tried anyway. At her laptop, she worked late into the night. She found writing about the things Carter had shown her effortless. It didn't seem to matter that the words weren't all that great. The experience...

Sky closed her laptop and sat back on the bed. They'd stayed at the bonfire until they were kicked out. Talking, laughing, even dancing silly to a couple of songs. No deadlines interrupted their night. Nothing more urgent than the moment.

The evening was the most enjoyable she'd had in months. Maybe longer.

The thought of leaving Monroe Falls, of leaving Carter, made her a bit melancholy. She had to remind herself that it was for the best. She'd done nothing but lie to him since the moment she met him. His trusting nature made Sky feel even worse. At least her name wasn't a lie.

If Carter had any suspicions at all, all he had to do was Google her. The headlines—mostly scandalous now—would fill his feed.

Tomorrow, Carter promised to take her fishing. And to the falls.

"I'll tell him the truth tomorrow, before any of that."

With the decision made, Sky set her laptop on the nightstand, and snuggled under the inn's quilt. Images of Carter's striking smile and his broad shoulders filling out his dark blue Carhartt shirt invaded her thoughts as she fell asleep.

---

The next morning, Sky was mildly disappointed to remember that Carter had an important client to meet, about a map of Maryland. Last night she'd been caught up in the bonfire, the people, and the opportunities for countless photos. *Should've asked Carter about his loves of maps.* Now she found herself insatiably curious.

He wore a brick wall exterior like an old, favorite jacket. But what did he hide behind that wall? She yearned to know.

She decided to roam the town, thankful she packed a pair of tennis shoes. But she hardly made it halfway down the staircase before Mrs. Bleeker intercepted her escape.

"Sky! Great news!"

From the elated glow on the woman's plump face, Sky would've believed Mrs. Bleeker just won a new car. "What's that, Mrs. Bleeker?"

"Lisa, please." But she didn't give Sky a chance

to correct herself. "Your editor called this morning. Your room's all taken care of!"

"That is wonderful news." Sky held her smile steadfast, relief flowing through her veins like a refreshing tonic. *Colleen.* Sky made a mental note to tease her friend later on about her magazine editor status. "Thank you for your patience too, Mrs. Bleeker." She thought about telling her she'd mention her stay at the Sleepy Inn, but something stopped her.

"Oh, Lisa, please!" Lisa reached below the counter. "Your editor sent this envelope for you as well. Wasn't sure if I should knock when it got here. Had it sent overnight. Must be important."

Sky smiled as she took the FedEx envelope, praying it held a bit of cash to get her by until she could get back and repay her best friend tenfold.

"And she mentioned the Sleepy Inn when she called. Our own paragraph in your article? Wow."

Sky raised an eyebrow at that. "Did she now?" *Great minds.*

"I have some time before I have to start lunch. You know, to answer any questions. Did you know we have a resident ghost?"

For the morning's remainder, Sky jotted notes and shot photos, all to Mrs. Bleeker's great pleasure. "Make sure you get my good side," she told Sky as she turned her hip toward the massive fireplace. "I can't believe I'm going to be in a magazine!"

Guilt crept in again, warning Sky she should

wrap this charade up before too many people in town got their hopes up. But to see such excitement buzzing in the woman's eyes, who was Sky to crush her dreams? After the weekend was over, she'd have to go back and face reality. This little sleepy town would forget she ever existed.

Carter would forget.

The thought made her heart plummet.

"I better drop my notes off upstairs. I still need to take some pictures downtown," she explained, having to clear her throat to hide the looming prick of depression. "I'll let you know if there're any more questions."

Sky couldn't get the door closed behind her fast enough. What was she doing? She'd never lied about anything like this in her life. She'd only been desperate for a place to lay low, and somehow that had backfired into a case of mistaken identity.

Shoving her camera in her purse, she forced herself not to run down the inn's stairs. If she could just get out and take a few photos, the world would calm around her again.

Though she'd only planned to head downtown, Sky wasn't surprised when her feet carried her to Main Street's storefront windows, to the same building whose roof had offered her a watching spot yesterday. From the sidewalk, the empty space called to her.

"It's really a great space."

The voice startled her, but soon Pam came into the reflection, blue eyes meeting her own in the glass. *Blue like Carter's.* "Has it been empty long?"

"Just a few months." Pam adjusted her fishing hat. "Lina Harrison had a quilting shop set up in there, but she retired and headed for Florida. Tired of our winters, I guess." Behind them, a car drove by. Pam waved. "You thinking of setting up shop somewhere?"

"I... I don't think... It's just that the magazine..." Sky hated how the lie tripped up her words. "I think it'd make a great photography studio," she said finally. Words were easier when they were true.

"That's where your heart really lies, isn't it, over journalism?"

Maybe it was their reflection in the window, oddly comforting on this warm fall day. "Yeah, it is." The easy way people recognized each other, and waved. Or the shuffle of leaves the wind ushered along behind cars on Main Street. Maybe it was simply the truth that wrung out in Pam's words.

Making partner didn't matter; she'd only wanted to please Elaine, to make her proud. But this, this was where her heart yearned to be.

Sky knew in that moment she no longer wanted to be a wedding planner. "Maybe it's time for a career change."

arter

"I hope you're not planning to hide in your office all day." Moose raised his head as Pam scolded Carter from the doorway.

He didn't look up. "After all that running around yesterday, I'm behind."

"I heard you promised to take Sky to the falls." His mom filled the doorway like a marble statue, sturdy, unmoving.

The last time they'd talked about a new woman in his life, Carter instantly went defensive. He expected his muscles to tense, his breathing to grow rigid. But when none of that happened, he looked up with a smile. "I did."

That caught Pam off guard. She stumbled over a reply; it didn't come.

"I wanted to finish up this Vermont map. I'm taking it home to hang."

"Before she comes over?"

"Precisely." Carter clipped a wire on the frame's back.

"And you're taking her fishing?"

"Can't say no to a beautiful woman who wants to go fishing, now, can I?"

Pam's eyebrow arched, and it was only now Carter realized her prized fishing hat wasn't sitting on her head, but resting in her hand. "What are you going to cook for dinner?"

"Dinner?"

Pam dropped her hat back on her mop of gray hair. "Can't expect a girl to spend a day with you and not feed her come evening." She tapped the doorframe on her way out of Carter's office. "It's a shame you can't convince her to stay in Monroe Falls."

Even Moose's eyes trailed after the footsteps as Pam descended the stairs. *Sky stay in Monroe Falls?* Carter wanted to shake the thought, shake the daydream. But a small voice was already nagging him to figure out a way to convince her to stay. Or at least, to come back.

———

"Don't look at me like that, Moose." The coonhound had been sitting quietly, attentively hoping for a handout at the kitchen island's side as Carter prepared marinade for the steaks. The longer he went without one, the more pitiful his big brown eyes grew. "You've got a perfectly good bowl of dog food with your name on it."

Maggie would've teased him about talking to the dog. The thought brought a faint smile. For the first time in as long as he could remember, the thought hadn't made him feel guilty. In his heart, he knew she'd want him to be happy again.

Sky arrived just before he sealed the foil packets of mixed vegetables.

"I don't think I've ever eaten dinner this early," she admitted, crossing the threshold. Moose trotted into the living room to the front door, his tail thumping against the doorframe. "Hey there, Moose!"

"I haven't put anything on the grill yet," Carter admitted, smiling at the way Sky knelt and greeted the dog with both hands rubbing his ears, the way Moose liked. "I thought we'd go fishing first. Eat when we get back." It was nearly four, and he wanted to ensure they caught the sunset tonight, out at the falls. It would make for a spectacular photo in her article, and a memory to treasure even if she decided not to come back.

Standing again, she asked, "We're not going to the football game?"

"Nah." Carter had avoided high school sports for years. Not because he wasn't supportive. He always bought whatever they were selling to raise money for new uniforms. He even donated a couple of items to their silent auction a couple of years back, raising funds for the kids to travel to the state basketball tournament. But crowds—he didn't care for them.

"You don't have any nephews or cousins or anything playing?"

The question struck him, clenching his chest. "My only sister passed almost a decade ago."

Sky's soft fingers curled around his arm, the scent of something like vanilla floating around him. "I'm so sorry, Carter." She dropped her hand before he could think of a next move. Somehow, they'd ended up in the kitchen. "Is there anything I can help with?"

"I think I have it all covered." He tossed a stray green bean to Moose. "Let's go fishing."

———

"Why maps?" Sky asked, casting her line. "What do you love about them?"

Carter had to repeat the question in his head to really digest the words. He'd been too caught up in watching her. Sky's easy way with baiting her hook and casting a line had him wondering how she'd really gone fifteen years without fishing.

"I've always loved maps," Carter said finally. "Something about the exploration. When I was little, I used to pretend I was Meriwether Lewis." He shook his head in disbelief that he was about to share such an intimate and partially embarrassing detail. But the story came out anyway. "I used to run along the river with a notepad and pencil, pretending to chart undiscovered territory. I wanted to travel the world."

"But you stopped."

"The maps started coming to me." Carter knew the answer was evasive, but how else did he tell the first woman he'd felt anything for since Maggie that he was too afraid to leave? Too afraid that his absence would only spell disaster for someone who needed him to stay close by?

"That's not the reason." She propped her pole against the cooler before scooting closer to him. Her hand rested on his arm. "Sometimes bad things happen, Carter. Things we can't control. But you can't let them keep you from doing what you love."

He stiffened, worried what this conversation might stir inside him. Sky meant well, he was certain. But he wasn't ready to let his guard down. *Not yet.* "I love working with maps. I— Hey, a bite."

Sky instantly reached for her pole, reeling in a

fighter. Carter waited for her to ask for his help, but she wrestled the little green guy up on her own.

"It's a brook trout."

She held the fish up by her line's end, preparing to unhook him. "How can you tell?"

"See those little red spots? On the belly? They've got that blue ring. Plus, it's a squaretail."

"Because rainbow have a forked tail."

*Marry this girl*, a voice whispered. Carter looked away while Sky unhooked the trout, kneeling in the boat as she gently lowered it back into the river. "Exactly."

Carter was certain he'd never seen anything more beautiful in his life.

CHAPTER 14

As the boat headed toward the falls, Sky couldn't help but think how Monroe Falls was charming her heart. Her whimsical side could picture a future here. And she'd squeeze in a bit of traveling. New England in the fall—what little she'd seen of it—was astounding. She swore the colorful leaves had deepened in their hues overnight: gold, orange the color of canned pumpkin, and crimson.

Carter steered the boat around a rock. "Is your older sister your only family back in Omaha?"

"Yeah." Sky let the motor's roar fill the silence that followed as she ignored Carter's intense gaze.

What would happen when she went back? She'd

worked so hard these past years to prove to Elaine that she could handle any responsibility. That she could be an integral part of a successful business. But now Sky didn't want to fight for the partnership. Or even the bonus. She just wanted out.

The boat slowed and Carter tied it off to a rickety-looking dock.

"What would you do if you could do anything?" Sky took his proffered hand. She could've climbed out on her own, despite the rocking, but something about that gesture brought her comfort. The tingles from the brush of his hand, something else entirely.

"This," Carter said when they were both firmly planted on the dock.

She smiled at that, a part of her heart glowing in their connected gaze. She longed to stay. *I could fall for Carter so easily.* Sky wanted him to fall for her. "There's nothing else you want?"

"Nope." He shook his head. "What about you?"

"To open my own photography studio." It was the first time she'd uttered the words out loud, but the confidence that came with them made her chest fill with butterflies. *Should I tell him the rest?* A cute little house on the edge of town, a studio in town where she'd take family portraits and senior pictures during the week. Shoot weddings on the weekends instead of plan them. Maybe spend her evenings wrapped in the arms of the man standing before her.

"Then you should." Something in his blue eyes,

bluer with the glint of setting sunlight, made her believe she could.

But she couldn't let herself get carried away. Not until she went home and faced the consequences. Until she made up with Elaine.

"So, we have to hike this little trail?" Sky nodded toward the steep and narrow dirt path littered with thick tree roots and boulders the size of small children.

"From here, it's the only way to the falls," Carter explained. "Most people drive, so this trail isn't the most maintained, but the state keeps it up just the same."

Sky noticed scattered orange trail markers, most spray painted on tree trunks or rocks along the way. She was certainly glad she'd worn her tennis shoes. She couldn't imagine hiking this rickety path in heeled boots.

Leading the way, she found herself oddly out of shape. Those spin classes she'd taken by the dozen at home had nothing on hiking straight uphill. She found herself reaching for a thin tree trunk, but her hand slipped before her foot found sturdy footing.

Carter caught her before she sent them both tumbling down the steep, rocky trail. His firm arms wrapped around her like a cocoon. For a moment, Sky couldn't breathe. She didn't want to hike to the falls or even back to the boat. She just wanted to relish in the safety she felt in these arms.

"Sky?" Carter's low voice said against her ear. "You okay to keep going? It's not too far."

The moment was shaken away, and Sky freed herself. "Yeah."

Her face flushed as she hiked forward, and she was careful to keep it hidden from Carter. Since the moment she showed up at his house, confusing thoughts had been flooding her mind. It felt like home, there in his kitchen watching him toss green beans to Moose. The concept of home, of building a life without someone, had been foreign to her for a long time. She'd been so focused on her own career...

From behind, Carter said, "I promise this little hike's worth the effort. There's this perfect lookout spot. It catches the setting sun against the falls. Right up there." He pointed to a dirt alcove less than fifty yards away. "If someone didn't know to look for it, they might miss it entirely."

As warned, the alcove was nearly overgrown. A tangle of branches above meant the state hadn't kept up regular maintenance. If that wasn't enough indication, the heavy, rusted chain with the "No One Beyond This Point" sign was.

"Are you sure this is okay?" Sky asked. "We're not going to get in trouble?" When the footsteps behind her stopped, she turned.

"Surely you don't get all your best pictures by following the rules?" he teased. "Seems like Journalism 101—sneaking across the off-limits lines."

There it was again, the mounting guilt for the lies she'd spun. She'd yet to set it right with Carter. Sky hopped over the low-hanging chain and continued into the overgrown alcove. "I've done my fair share of trespassing for a good photo." But when Sky thought back, it had been years since she made photography a priority.

"You're frowning," Carter observed. "That's not usually the reaction people have out here."

"I forgot my camera. In the boat—"

"You're in town a couple more days, right?" Carter asked. "We can come back out tomorrow. Tonight, just enjoy the view." He took her hand, tingles from the contact racing up her arm. He led her to the rickety-looking wooden railing. "I certainly am."

Before Sky could turn, he wrapped an arm around her chest and pulled her back from the untrustworthy barrier. "You don't want to lean on it. It's mostly rotted."

Sky peeked over the railing, all too aware of the beating of his heart against her back. The drop wasn't quite straight down, but the water was at least thirty feet below them, the path littered with jutting tree roots and jagged boulders, half buried in the dirt. But when she lifted her head to follow the waterfall's hiss, her gaze caught the golden rays of light shimmering off the falls.

"This is the only place you can see it quite like this," Carter said.

"Like a little best-kept secret."

"I'm hoping if you put it in your article, the state'll decide on repairs. This railing. Open up the path again. It's too beautiful here for people not to know about it."

Sky turned then, meeting Carter's eyes. A blue that could be her undoing. "You'd share such a quiet, hidden spot with the world?"

"I know. Doesn't sound like me."

"No, not really. Not the anti-social, reclusive Carter Jensen I've come to know."

"Okay, so maybe I'm making that up." His expression broke into a mischievous smile. "Truth is, I don't want to share my special spot with anyone. Never thought I would. Until you showed up."

She overcame her instinct to lean a hand on the rail and grabbed for his elbow instead. Carter's words, spoken with such conviction, had her legs wobbling. What could that possibly mean? They'd just met, she wasn't staying... But a moment later when his lips met hers, she surrendered without a fight. He kissed her softly, as if asking for permission.

Sky reached for his cheek and pulled him closer, magic sparking at the kiss that spun her world sideways. Had she ever been kissed in a place as beautiful as this? At sunset?

She didn't think so.

Carter's hand combed through her thick hair, drawing her face closer, their kiss deepening until the world became a blur of dizzy stars. Sky's heart raced erratically as her hands found the back of his neck. In this moment, she never wanted to go back to Omaha. She wanted to stay here, to see where things might go with Carter.

She wanted a new life entirely.

arter

He'd kissed other women since Maggie. Not many, but a couple. Enough to know that kissing Sky was nothing like kissing any of those other women. It was something as rare as the antique maps he hunted.

Carter warned himself not to think too much about what it could mean.

"Can't remember the last time I've been able to see this many stars," Sky said in awe, her eyes upturned to the night sky. "So beautiful."

"You don't normally write articles on smaller places?" Carter asked, certain she'd traveled to at least a couple of locales that offered the same view.

"Um, no."

Her reserved answer stirred a warning, but he shoved it away. Maybe he was careless to let one simple kiss—okay, who was he kidding, one earth-shattering kiss—cloud his judgment. But he didn't care. For once, he was living purely in the moment, and it felt wonderful.

He steered the boat to his dock and tied it down. "Let's go have some dinner out under the stars."

He offered his hand to help her, sensing a hesitation in her reluctant silence. But tonight he wouldn't press.

"It is a little chilly out," he admitted, joining her on the dock. "Maybe dinner inside. But while it's cooking, I do have a warm blanket and a really comfortable lounge chair. Perfect for watching the stars."

She hadn't dropped his hand as they walked toward the house. Moose appeared in the upstairs window. Normally, Carter would've brought him along to the falls, but he hadn't wanted to risk his curiosity capsizing the boat. Not with Sky's expensive camera. There was something oddly normal about this scene—Sky at his side, Moose eagerly awaiting their return.

"Well, since you have a warm blanket and all."

"Hard to say no to a good blanket."

---

Out on the deck, Carter fired up the grill, then dragged the fire pit from the corner and filled it with stray pieces of wood.

It was foolish, he knew, to spend time with Sky for reasons outside of her article and what it could do for Darcy's—even for Monroe Falls. But he hadn't felt this way around another woman in years. Even if Sky were leaving when the weekend was over, at least it gave him hope.

Maybe there was someone else out there for him. Maybe it was okay to want that.

"A fire too?" Sky slid the door closed behind her. "All you need are s'mores, and you won't get me to leave!"

Carter couldn't remember the last time he'd even thought to make s'mores over a fire, but he suddenly wished he'd had the forethought to pick up the ingredients at Mason's Market earlier today. "I don't have those, but I could get you a cup of hot chocolate while the steaks cook?"

"That sounds perfect."

At the door, Carter watched her unfold the blanket and take up one corner on the lounge loveseat, leaving room for him.

He swallowed.

Moose trotted out before he could close the door. Carter heard Sky talking to the coonhound. It made him smile, despite the shaky hands that prepared her hot chocolate.

Out on the deck, handing Sky her cup, the graze of her fingers made his breath catch. He wanted nothing more than to abandon the steaks and wrap her in his arms. Hold her close, outside beneath the stars.

"How long before dinner?"

"Not long." He trotted back to the kitchen, retrieving the steaks and veggies from the fridge. Once they were situated on the grill, he took the seat next to her. When she tossed half the blanket across his lap, he was forced to close the gap between them in order for the blanket's edge to cover his legs. Before he could talk himself out of it, he'd draped an arm over her shoulder and pulled her against him. His reward: Sky leaning her head against his shoulder, the vanilla scent of her shampoo reaching him.

"Could stay out here all night," she said between small sips. "Just stargaze. You've got a beautiful place. Have you always lived here?"

"I built the house right before Maggie and I got married."

He felt her head turn, her face angled at his. "*You* built it?"

The temptation to taste the hot cocoa on her lips was too much. He gave her a gentle kiss, releasing her slowly. "Not by myself, no. I had some help. But I did that before Darcy's. Construction. Building houses, mostly."

"You miss it?"

"Not really," Carter said. "I still do quite a bit of handy work for people in town. But finding old maps and books is what I love doing. Maps, in particular. You get to see what places looked like in a different point in history. It's kind of like being transported back in time."

"That does sound wondrous."

They sat that way, curled around each other beneath the blanket with the fire roaring and Moose at their feet, until the steaks were ready.

———

Carter spent the entire meal rambling about the origins of Darcy's and the quirky uniqueness of what it offered. And internally chiding himself. Probably overcompensating for nerves. He'd not found himself this skittish since high school.

"I love that name—Huck's Hideaway." Sky set her fork down and nudged him with her shoulder. "Perfect name for a room filled with banned books. That's clever."

"I thought so."

"Wait, *you* came up with that one?"

"Is it that hard to believe that I came up with *one* name?"

Sky turned in her barstool, her face only inches away. "You're full of surprises, Carter Jensen." She leaned closer, hesitating only a moment before reaching for his neck. The kiss at the falls had nothing on the kiss now. He felt dizzy in the best way.

"What would it take, Sky?" he whispered. "What would it take to make you stay?"

As if snapped from a trance, Sky froze. "I—I have to go." She slipped from his arms and fled. Moose barked from the kitchen.

"Sky, wait!"

"I—I'll come back in the morning."

When Carter made it to the front door, Sky was already halfway down his drive. He watched her run until she reached the main road into town where he knew she'd be safe. It wasn't until that moment that he let himself wonder, *What just happened?*

ky

Sky had every intention of telling Carter the truth over dinner. But there in his arms, the world finally felt calm. And right. If all she had out of this weekend was that one solitary memory, it would be enough to get her through whatever consequences she faced. But then he asked her to stay.

She couldn't do it. She couldn't. And she certainly couldn't keep lying to him. It'd been a fitful night without any real sleep. Today, the lying had to stop.

The walk to Darcy's from the inn was far too short. Sky wanted a few more moments to relish in the memory of Carter's embrace. His kiss. The safety and comfort she felt with him. It all stirred something deep she'd never felt before, and that frightened her most of all.

Stepping onto Darcy's porch, Sky noted Pam's empty rocking chair. Probably best that she wasn't here to witness Sky leaving in tears. Because what else could she expect when the truth came out?

Colleen had already booked her flight back to Omaha. In an hour, a car would pick her up from the Sleepy Inn. It'd be easier to hide in her room until then. At least, she thought so at first, but Sky couldn't do that to Carter. She couldn't leave that way. He deserved better. He deserved the truth.

"Sky, good morning!" Lucy greeted. "Can I fix you a cup?"

Sky shook her head. "No thanks, Lucy. I just need to talk to Carter. Is he here?"

"Upstairs. On the phone with a client."

The same little table by the window that had beckoned Sky three days earlier sat empty now. She slipped onto the wobbly chair, her back to the noisy group of elderly ladies in the opposite corner. They probably thought she'd want to interview Darcy's regulars. One at a time, they shot glances her way. If they got word of her little confession, it'd be all over town before Sky left. *What would Lisa think then?* If Sky could spare herself that one embarrassment, she'd make it through this.

At the creaking of the stairs, Sky's head shot up.

"Sky." Carter stood, hands shoved into the pockets of his jeans. The sunlight danced off his shoulders, illuminating confusion in his blue eyes even from across the room. "I was worried about you."

A couple of the ladies poked their heads up in a perfect imitation of hens. Dark noises joined the glances they pointed her way. But Sky rose, turned her back, and bravely approached Carter. "I have something I need to tell you."

He reached out, two firm hands resting on her forearms, ignoring the clucking behind them. "Sky, what's wrong?"

She pulled back, her eyes closing as she took a deep breath and locked the memory of his touch away for safe keeping.

"Sky, you're worrying me."

The gaggle of women hadn't gone back to conversing in their usual quiet, dull roar. Sky ignored them. "Carter, I haven't been honest with you."

"What do you mean?"

The gaggle grew more clamorous as it surrounded them. Over it all, an uneasy feeling settling in the pit of Sky's stomach.

"Ladies, please." Carter looked up the stairs, but thought better of it, it seemed. "Can you give us—"

"I'm not a travel writer," Sky blurted, nothing careful or considered after all.

"I don't understand."

"I'm a... wedding planner."

"Ha!" one of the tough birds clucked. "More like a *homewrecker*! Carter, what do you make of this?" She held up a magazine, waving it like a flag.

The full page picture displayed an unflattering shot of Ken kissing Sky. Only, the headline implied the opposite:

**Wedding planner breaks up Omaha's happiest couple minutes before "I dos"**

"Carter, it's not how it looks." Sky stood at the base of the stairs, tears filling her eyes. "If I could just explain—"

He looked as if he was being swallowed up in a crowd of panic. His gaze swept the room as he searched frantically for an escape route. "I have to go." He pushed his way through, knocking the tabloid to the ground as he stomped off to the front door and left Sky with her heart puddled on the floor.

"Don't you dare go after him," one woman warned. "He deserves better than the likes of *you*."

arter

"What do you mean, she's gone?" Carter asked Mrs. Bleeker Saturday afternoon.

"She checked out two hours ago. Said, 'Thanks for everything, Lisa, but I have a flight to catch.'"

It was obvious from the innkeeper's calm response that the news hadn't reached her yet. It'd only be a matter of time, and Carter didn't want to be the one to break it to her. "Did she leave her phone number?"

"I'm afraid not." Mrs. Bleeker studied him hard and primly reminded, "Seems if she wanted you to have it, Carter, she'd have given it to you."

There was harsh truth in those words. Carter

couldn't peg for a moment what had really brought Sky Emerson to Monroe Falls, but he knew he wasn't ready to never see her again. He didn't believe she was really capable of breaking up a wedding.

And now the woman he'd grown so fond of the past few days was gone without so much as a good-bye note. Without the chance to see what they might become.

The tears that had lingered in her eyes moments before he fled Darcy's haunted him. Denying her the chance to explain her side of the story... he'd let someone else down.

Carter did what he always did when he needed time to think.

He went fishing.

## CHAPTER 18

Sky

Sky, emotionally exhausted, knew exactly what she had to do when the plane touched down in Omaha on Saturday night. Colleen's offer to share a bottle of wine sounded wonderful, but she had to talk to Elaine.

"Are you sure, honey?" Colleen asked during their call after Sky deplaned. "It can't wait till tomorrow?"

"I already asked Elaine to pick me up." Sky had no more than stepped outside when she spied her sister's Escalade pull up along baggage claim. "Gotta go."

"Call me."

"I will. And thanks. For everything."

"If you don't call, I *will* show up. Just to make sure Elaine hasn't hacked you into little pieces."

"Love you, Coll."

Elaine didn't budge from the vehicle, not to Sky's surprise. She steadied herself with a deep breath before setting her suitcase in the back seat. She let the car door fall shut and braced her hand on the front door's handle. With a quick count to five, she fell into the passenger seat. Elaine didn't look at her. She simply eased out into the snaggle of airport traffic and headed for the main road back into town.

"I'm sorry," Sky said.

"Sorry, huh?" Elaine's tone was laced with the acid Sky expected. "You *disappeared* on me, Skylar. Sorry doesn't give me back all the sleep I lost trying to find you."

Despite the venomous, motherly tone, Sky hid a small, touched smile. She expected Elaine to lash out, but about the ruined wedding and lost future clients. "I thought it'd be better for me to lay low. Better for your business."

Elaine whipped a left turn at a yellow light. "You were wrong about that. But right about *him*."

"Maybe— Wait, what?"

"Ken Stovermeyer—governor's nephew or not—is a total lowlife."

Sky chuckled at Elaine's use of the insult. *Someone's been online.* It didn't fit the prestigious and well-put-together appearance her sister wore even now, in her designer pencil skirt and heels, on her day off. "Yeah. Well—"

"I'm sorry."

"What?" Sky turned her entire torso toward Elaine. Was this really her older sister talking? "What would *you* have to be sorry about?"

"I should've listened. Eight months ago, you told me not to take them on."

"But they were your highest paying clients from two prestigious political families," Sky argued, despite how backwards this all felt. Sky quoted her sister, from the day Elaine decided to take them on. "They were going to rake in clients for years to come."

"Doesn't mean I should've sacrificed my principles. I could see it too, that they didn't want to get married. But I chose to ignore it."

As they rolled up to a stoplight in the midst of downtown Omaha, Sky felt herself mourning Monroe Falls and its complete lack of stoplights. Its complete lack of traffic, four-lane roads, and smothering skyscrapers. She imagined Carter cursing at all the people here, the thought squeezing her heart.

"But *you*—you've got a real gift, Sky." At the next stoplight, Elaine dug in her purse and tossed an envelope at Sky.

"What's this?"

"Your bonus."

"But—"

"You've earned it. Every penny."

For a moment, Sky was filled with elation. After five years of busting her tail for Elaine, she'd finally recognized her worth. But the moment quickly dissipated. "I'm not coming back to Catching the Bouquet, Elaine."

"Don't be ridiculous. Of course you are. I'm making you partner. It's what you've always dreamed about."

Sky shook her head, waiting for another stoplight so Elaine could meet her eyes. "Actually, it's not."

"I don't understand."

"Elaine, this is *your* dream. And I wanted so much to make you proud that..." She stopped. Tears dropped as she imagined the anguish happening inside Elaine right now. "I didn't realize that until this weekend." Which only made Sky think of Carter and the hurt she'd seen laced in his confused eyes when he ran out of Darcy's at the heartbreak she caused him.

"What *do* you want, Skylar?"

Sky steeled herself, remembering the same words she said to Carter. They were harder to voice now—here, back in reality. Back in her actual life. Perhaps it was only a whimsical dream, and she should take Elaine up on her offer before it was off the table.

"Sky?"

"I want to open a photography studio."

"I see."

They drove in strained silence until they reached Sky's apartment complex. Elaine shifted the SUV into park. It was her turn to turn fully and face Sky.

"Skylar, you know I love you no matter what, right?" She reached for Sky's hand and squeezed. "If you want to open a photography studio, then you should."

"Really?"

"Absolutely."

Sky threw her arms around Elaine and hugged her sister to near suffocation. Tears soaked both their shoulders. "I'm sorry, Elaine. I'm sorry I ran off. Sorry I ignored most of your texts."

"You should be, you know." The motherly scolding returned to Elaine's tone.

Sky narrowed her eyes, fully aware that the playful edge of her stare was evident. "Well, you *did* freeze my accounts."

"Yeah. Well, there's that."

"Elaine!"

"Next time, tell me where you're going. Promise me, Sky."

"I promise."

arter

It'd been two months since Sky left Monroe Falls. Carter could admit to himself that he still felt miserable.

He'd been horrible company at Lucy's family dinner yet again, this time deciding to show himself out to the back deck to relieve the others of his brooding.

After her departure, Carter dug up every article he could find about Sky Emerson. Turned out there was more to the story than the first tabloid let on, including several follow-up stories about the groom using his wedding planner. From the number of confessional articles from Ken Stovermeyer, Carter could see how the jerk used Sky as a publicity stunt to get out of his arranged wedding and gain a modicum of internet fame and no doubt future voters.

Carter heard footsteps behind him before he saw the shadow fall over the back yard. He didn't look up. Morose, he stated, "I should be mad at her, you know. For lying."

"But you aren't," Mom said.

"No." In the weeks she'd been gone, Carter had tried to move on. He'd even gone on a couple of dates, convinced Sky had only briefly entered his life to encourage him to find happiness again. But those dates had ended abruptly, because Sky Emerson wasn't the one sitting across the table.

"So, Carter, why are you sitting here?"

"What am I supposed to do?"

"Forgive her."

Carter looked up at his mom, bundled up in her winter coat. She hated the cold, yet here she was standing outside with him in the snow, giving him advice. It had to mean something. "I know she wasn't lying about everything. She wasn't lying about *most* things. No woman makes up a story about loving to fish, then drops a red worm on a hook as easily as breathing."

Mom laughed in her warm, hearty style. "Now, how can you forget a girl that like?"

"What should I do?"

"Go after her."

"But I can't leave. What if—"

"Carter, I love you. But you have to stop living in fear."

The words caught in his throat, but Carter didn't choke them down this time. They had to be spoken. "Every time I leave, something happens. Someone needs me, and I'm not here. How can I go chasing after some woman who didn't even leave me her number?"

"Life will happen no matter where you are, and you have to let it." Mom patted him on the shoulder. "It's cold out here. Go get your girl, Carter."

ky

Sky watched the movers pack her final box in the apartment she'd shared with her best friend for the past three years, and yet she didn't feel sad. Instead, for the first time since she returned home she felt excited. Her heart had ached for Carter every night for weeks, but each day without him helped her let go, or so she told herself.

*I don't deserve him.*

Her phone buzzed, and Sky lit up, seeing who was calling. "Mabel! I hope you've got good news." Turned out Mabel Clancy, a writer for *Travel Often*, was a good friend of the Stovermeyer family. The favor had been an easy one to beg off of Kenny's mother in exchange for Sky's refusal to talk to any press.

"My editor *loves* your photos, Sky."

"So, you're going to run the story?"

"Of course! You gave me such great notes to work with, that whipping up an article was no problem at all. Besides, we all know everyone will be ogling the pictures anyway."

"When will it run?"

"Next edition."

Sky's heart swelled. She'd have Colleen call Lisa Bleeker with the news; she was sure to spread it around town. Sky wanted to call Carter, but she couldn't bring herself to. She'd hurt him, disappointed him. It wasn't fair to selfishly want to hear his voice.

"Thank you, Mabel. I can't tell you how much this means."

"I'm supposed to let you know," Mabel added, "my editor Janet will be calling you—about a job."

"What?"

"We need a photographer on staff. She loved your take on the small Vermont town, and we don't have anyone currently in the area. Does traveling around New England sound like your kind of thing?"

Tears of happiness welled. "It sounds perfect!"

Sky erupted into a silly dance, spinning in a circle until she was dizzy. Then she nearly tripped when she saw who was standing in her doorway.

"Carter."

"Hey."

"How did you get in?" But the answer was obvious even before she asked it. *Colleen.*

"Sky Emerson, you're a hard woman to track down."

"You're not in Monroe Falls." It was like looking at a hallucination. *It has to be.* The Carter Jensen she'd come to know, even in so short a time, would never travel this far from home. Not even for the rarest map.

"That's because *you're* not in Monroe Falls."

Sky swallowed, hoping tears wouldn't betray her. "Why'd you come?"

Carter took a few steps toward her, then stopped. "Did you not want me to?"

*Of course I did.* She'd dreamed about it nearly every night since she left. Always wondering what it'd be like for a man she pined after to show up at her doorstep. "I can't believe you came all this way."

Carter closed the distance between them, hesitating when he seemed to see the apartment for the first time, noticing how empty it was aside from a select few pieces of furniture that would stay behind. "You're moving?"

Sky shrugged and tucked her phone into her back pocket. "Something like that. Look, Carter—"

"Where are you going?"

Sky swallowed, keeping her gaze on the leather

sofa the movers had yet to retrieve, and safely averted from Carter. "I haven't really figured that out yet. Thought I'd do a little traveling until I found a good spot."

"Oh."

Bravely, she looked up. Her pulse raced at his intense gaze. "I don't expect you to understand. I lied to you, and if you can't forgive me for that, I get it. It was an awful thing to do. I don't expect you to want anything to do with me, even if you've tracked me down to chew me out for letting everyone down."

Suddenly he was standing in front of her again, hands on her shoulders. "Are you kidding? I'm crazy about you, Sky."

The words caused her legs to falter, and she felt thankful the back of her sofa was there to keep her from toppling. "You are? Wait—that's a *good* crazy, right?"

"Yes." The corner of his mouth lifted. "Come back with me, Sky. Come back with me to Monroe Falls. I know a certain storefront that would make the perfect photography studio."

A tear of disbelief and joy fell down her cheek. "I don't know. Are—are you sure?"

"Sky, I can't get you out of my head. I feel something, something *real* here." He placed the palm of her hand against his chest, the rapid beats thumping against her fingers. "Don't you?"

She'd missed him. Ached for more nights curled

up together beneath the stars. "I know I want to find out."

Carter tucked a stray hair behind her ear, his warm hand cupping the back of her neck. "I want nothing more than to see your smile every day. My world has been a dark and lonely place without it."

"But I lied to you, Carter. I lied to everyone. What will the town say? They'll never forgive me."

"Please, then why did Mrs. Bleeker tell me that *Travel Often*'s printing an article next month—about Darcy's and Monroe Falls?"

"How—" Sky laughed at that, no longer shocked that news had traveled so fast. "Is nothing a secret in that town?"

"Nothing. Not even the way I feel about you."

He drew her lips to his. The kiss made her dizzy and her heart full. She wasn't sure if she was in love with Carter, but Sky very much wanted to find out if she could be. "Okay," she said between kisses.

"Okay?" Carter's forehead rested against hers, both a little breathless.

"I'll come back with you."

ky

*Three months later...*

Sky walked her last clients of the day to the door of her Monroe Falls studio, catching Carter walking toward her from his truck. She'd opened her doors to her own private photography studio only last week, and already was booked solid. Turned out having The Hens on one's good side had its perks.

"Looks like another successful day, if their smiles are any indication." He greeted her with a long, slow kiss that made her toes curl. Yes, moving to Monroe

Falls had been one of the best decisions she ever made.

Moose poked his head through the open passenger window of the running truck. Snow still coated the ground, but Vermont, Sky found, was beautiful any time of the year. "You all packed?"

"I am." Carter kissed her once more. "The question is are *you*?"

Sky slipped on her coat and turned down the lights. "For once, I am."

"Then, Maine, here we come."

The smile that spread across her lips stretched her cheeks. Never in a hundred years would Sky have guessed she and Carter would be traveling together like this. Sky on assignment for the magazine, and Carter in pursuit of some priceless map. This man, he owned her entire heart.

Before they parted ways at the front of the truck, Sky pulled on Carter's arm and spun him around to face her. "Have I told you lately that I love you?"

"Not since this morning." He wrapped her in his arms, kissing her once more in the lightly falling snow. "I love you, Sky Emerson. I'm so glad you decided to take a chance on Monroe Falls. On me." He kissed her again.

Moose gave an approving bark from the truck, tail wagging. Seemed he too was excited about all the future adventures that awaited them.

## ~THE END~

Sign up for Jacqueline's Newsletter to be notified about current projects and new releases!

**Love cowboys, sweet romances, and small towns? Check out The Starlight Cowboys series!**

Cowboys & Starlight (Book 1)

Cowboys & Firelight (Book 2)

Cowboys & Sunrises (Book 3)

Cowboys & Moonlight (Book 4)

Cowboys & Mistletoe (Book 5)

Jacqueline Winters has been writing since she was nine when she'd sneak stacks of paper from her grandma's closet and fill them with adventure. She grew up in small-town Nebraska and spent a decade living in beautiful Alaska. She writes sweet contemporary romance and contemporary romantic suspense.

She's a sucker for happily ever after's, has a sweet tooth that can be sated with cupcakes, and believes sangria was possibly the best invention ever. On a relaxing evening, you can find her at her computer writing her next novel with her faithful dog poking his adorable head out from beneath her desk.